E11o
MOM

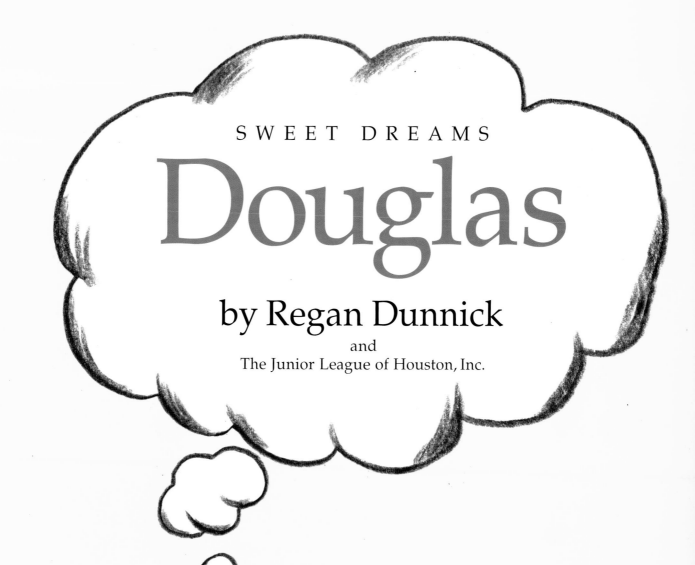

SWEET DREAMS

Douglas

by Regan Dunnick

and

The Junior League of Houston, Inc.

The Junior League of Houston, Inc., is an organization of women committed to promoting voluntarism, developing the potential of women, and improving communities through the effective action and leadership of trained volunteers. Its purpose is exclusively educational and charitable.

Also by The Junior League of Houston, Inc.:
Stop and Smell the Rosemary: Recipes and Traditions to Remember (1996)
The Star of Texas Cookbook (1983)
Houston Junior League Cookbook (1968)

First Printing September 2002, 20,000 copies

Library of Congress Cataloging in Publication Data main entry under title
Sweet Dreams Douglas
2002103988

ISBN # 0-9632421-3-X

Printed in China

Any inquiries about this book or orders for additional copies should be directed to:
The Junior League of Houston, Inc.
1811 Briar Oaks Lane
Houston, Texas 77027
800-432-2665
www.juniorleaguehouston.org

Mom, can I jump 'til
I get sleepy?

Douglas, please!

Peek-a-boo?

Douglas!

Read another story?

I've already read three.

Tickle me?

*Douglas,
we've done that.*

Another glass
of water?

No!

*Now Douglas,
go to sleep... sweet dreams.*

Excuse me sir,
do you dream?

Why yes, I dream of reaching the yummiest leaves at the top of the tree.

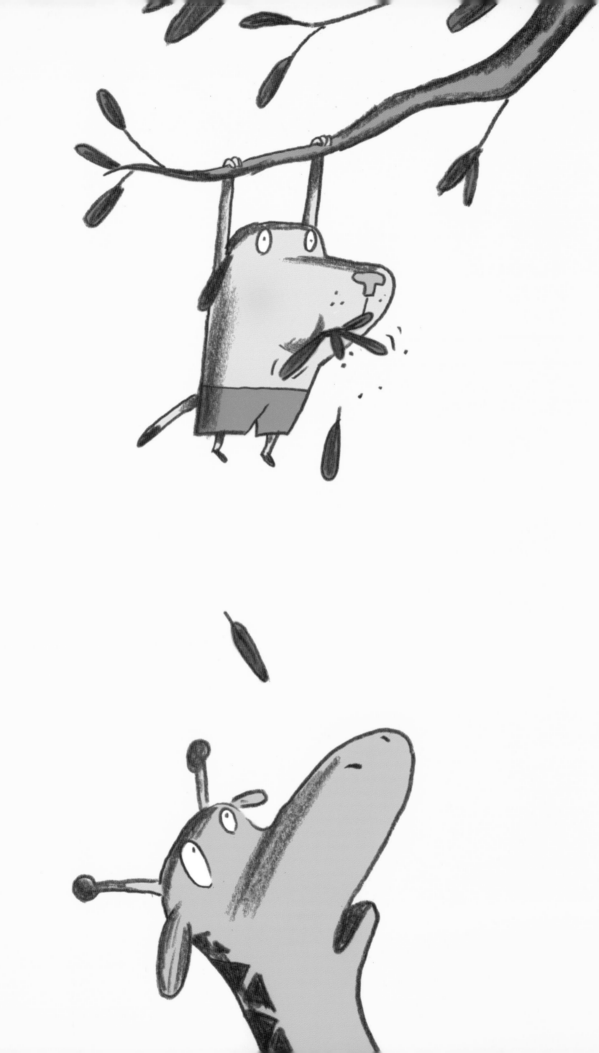

Do you dream,
Miss Butterfly?

*Of course!
I dream of landing
in a field of
fragrant flowers.*

Phew,
my getaway!

Big fish, do you dream?

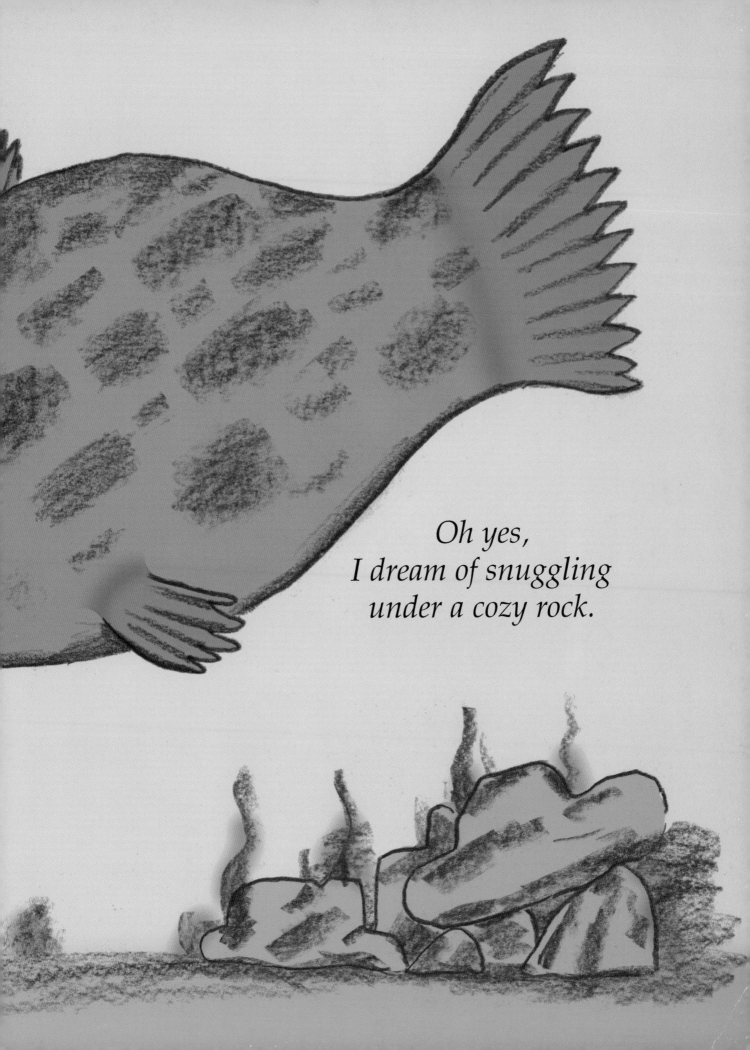

Oh yes,
I dream of snuggling
under a cozy rock.

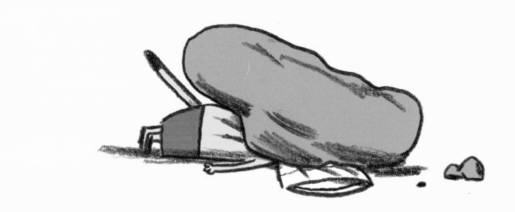

I'm still not sure I dream!
Do any of you?

I dream of meeting the queen.

... of coming out of my shell, of course.

... a pastrami and fly sandwich, please.

... a carrot castle for me!

Howdy!

Eeek!

Yuk!

Ugh!

What about you... do chameleons dream?

Hmmm…

I'm so glad you asked!
I was just dreaming
of changing my color and
taking a wild ride!

Look little one, you have to dream
your own dreams. They can be as simple as
something you want to do or become.
It's not how or what you dream… just dream.

Just dream?

Hooray for Douglas!

Dream Readers Book Club

The Junior League of Houston, Inc., extends heartfelt thanks to the Dream Readers Book Club members who generously supported this project from the early stages. Their memberships helped underwrite the initial production costs for *Sweet Dreams Douglas* and demonstrated a commitment to literacy and reading. Thank you for helping us realize this dream!

Magical Dreamers

Nicole Lanier Abib*
Ben Atnipp
Julia Atnipp
Sarah Atnipp
Will Atnipp
Emily & Scott Brown
Gillian & Caitlin Connelly
Caroline Cowan*
Griffin Cowan
Michael Cowan
Carson Crain
Philip Crain
Baker*, Brooks & Sterling Elias
Grace Fraser
Will Fraser*
Laurel Halliburton
Amanda Hansen
Alex Herrera*
Catherine Herrera*
H. John Herrera*
Anderson Calvert Mohle
Olivia Greer Mohle*
Theodore Westerfield Mohle, IV
Jeff, Claire & Ellie Pena
Candice Reilly*
Therese Reilly
Thomas Reilly
Allison Sprague*
Andrew Sprague
Coco Sprague
Emmy Sprague*
Phin Sprague*
Anne & Michael Stewart
Caroline Stewart
Todd Terreson
Virginia Terreson

Nicholas & Katherine Whalley
Hallie Kathleen Wilson*
Macon Fitzgerald Wilson*
Seagren Elizabeth Wilson*

Whimsical Dreamers

Mr. & Mrs. David Abney & Family
Laura & Sarah Aldridge
Elizabeth Lovell Allen
Emily Clare Anderson*
John James Clayton Anderson
Lawton Anderson*
Jeanie, David & Georgia Arnold
Austin Askew
Jake Askew
Sam Askew
Evans Attwell, II
Mary Evans Attwell
Patrick Attwell
Petersen Attwell
Family of Mary and Evans Attwell
Abigail Avery*
Paige Avery*
Caitlin Bailey
Clare Bailey
Jack Bailey*

Christine D. Balkum
Denise "Deannie" Heppler Balkum
The Barazi Family
Hamilton Chase Tripp Barnett*
Caroline Elizabeth Barrett*
Jack Elliott Barrett
The Rick Beeler Family
Jenifer, Eli & Joshua Ben-Shoshan
Charles Harrison Bennett
Carl Scott Bernicker*
Lily Daphne Bernicker*
The Todd Binet Family
Alex Blackburn
The Bob Blades Family
Katherine Lenoir Blunk
John Stafford Boland
Beau and Jack Brady
Murphy J. Brennan*
Jack Allen Brenner*
Walt Bruce, Jr.
Allison Burbach
Michael Burbach
Caroline Burke
Thomas Burke
Walter Burke
Anne Camille Cagle
John Busch Cagle
Andrew D. Campbell*
William J. Campbell, Jr.*
Elizabeth Anne Carl*
Virginia Fay Carl*
Cooper Carlyle*
Connor Carrigan
Virginia Cates
Catherine Chandler
Gary Chandler
Grant Chandler*
Grayson Chandler*
Christian Charbonnet*
Elizabeth Anne Charbonnet
Taylor Charbonnet*
The Cisarik Family
Henry Rogan Clark*
Katherine Scott Clearman*
Story Clements*
The Clutter Family
Kevin Cole
Matthew Cole*
Jeremy Graeme Colvin*
Justin Nathaniel Colvin*
Caroline Connell*
Michael Connell*
Will Connell*
Alexandra Lynn Cook
Laurel Marie Cook
Mary Katherine Cooper
Channing Rebecca Corbett*
Reagan Alexandra Corbett*
Tinsley Elizabeth Corbett*
Teddy Crane
Michael Travis Crittenden
Brock Culwell
Stasie Culwell
Sarah Kathryn Cunningham
Claire Emily Dameris
Elizabeth Ann Dameris
James Davies
Madeline Davies
Daniel Bennett Davis
G. Trevor Davis, Jr.*
John Aubrey Davis
Laura Grace Davis*
Matthew Lawrence Davis
Andrew DeWalch
Binz DeWalch
Meredith W. Dickson*
Morgan B. Dickson*
Garrett Diehl
The David Dominy Family
Andrew Shearman Donaldson
Parker Howland Donaldson*
Charles Andrew Dorfman*
Claire Louise Dorfman*
Lyndsay Elizabeth Dow*
Michael Douglas Dow*

Julia Michelle Dubose
Coleman DuCharme*
Willy DuCharme
Andrew Duenner
Kaki Duenner
Kelly Morrell Duenner
Stuart Duenner
William Ashley Edens, Jr.*
Mary Ann Enerson
Benjamin Thomas Enos
Elizabeth Gay Entrekin
Emily Anne Entrekin*
Katie Erikson
Ryan Erikson
Harrison "Bradley" Erwin
Henry "Blair" Erwin
Amelia Eskridge*
Evan & Kylie Fichter*
Clay, Carrie & Kelly Fisher*
Caroline Fitzgerald
Davis Flowers
Noah Flowers
Rebecca Flowers*
Lucy Maas Frankfort*
Rachael Frantz*
Caroline Frantz*
Grace Frantz*
Kristin Frantz
Grant Fuechec
Taylor Fuechec*
Ava Marlane Fulweber
James Adair Fulweber
Hank Funderburk*
Catherine Elizabeth Fusillo
William Henry Fusillo
Anneysa Beatrice Gaille
Sydney Gauss
Margaret Gee
Tom & Michele Gee
Allison Giblin*
Mariah Giblin*
Elizabeth Gibson*
Marion Gibson
Victoria Gibson*
Lewis Henry Gissel IV
Caitlyn Gold*
Jessica Gold*
Mary Esther Gonzalez
Stephen Gonzalez
Doyle Alex Graham, III
Frances Lawren Graham
Isabelle Alexandra Graham
Daniel Grant
Harrison Grant
Jordan Grant
Davis Gray*
Sheldon Gray*
John Robert Greenwalt
Miranda Greenwalt
Jenny Greer*
Ginny Griffin*
Joe Griffin
Will Griffin, III*
Bebe Griffith
Ali Lockwood Gundry
Molly Grace Gundry
Elyse Haberman
Ryan Haberman
Cienna Hancock*
Saxon Hancock*
Anna Lauren Hanhausen
Madison Kate Hann*
Morgan Kent Hann*
The Kelly Harris Family
Edward Bolin Heard, Jr.
Austin & Benjamin Henderson
Madison Hayley Henderson
Kathryn Hoppe
Miller Humphreys*
Jordan Leigh Jackson*
Victoria Barry Jackson*
James Lee Jacobe Family
Kendrick II, Keller, Carson & Cameron James
Tany & Kendrick James
Mayme J. John

John Morgan Johnson, IV
Katherine Adelle Johnson*
Stephen & Amber Johnson*
Dr. Frances M. Jones
Shelby Faville Stephens Jordan*
Amy Caylin Keliehor
James Carson Keliehor
Maxwell Coffman Keliehor
Mary Alex Khater
Nicholas Khater*
Noah Khater
Colleen Kilroy*
Lauren Rudd Kirk*
Atticus Koch
Connor Kenneth Kolb*
Courtney Lauren Kolb
Anna-William Hagle Kornberg
Eleanor-Day Hagle Kornberg
Mark Edward Laborde
Alexander Grant Landowski
London Lane*
Jacob Gregory Lawyer
James ("J.D.") Leaverton
Mikayla Leaverton
William Gentry Lee, III
Fallin Leger*
Alyson Lembcke
Peyton Levy*
Sellars Levy*
Anna, John & James Lilly*
Christopher Lindsey*
Olivia Grace Lindsey
Shelby Diane Little*
Avery McGlasson Looser
Elizabeth Brock Looser*
Caroline Mitchell Love
Catherine May Love
Mary Catherine Love
Cooper Whitmore Lueck
Landon Wheeler Lueck
Caroline Kramer Lum*
William DeLorenzo Lum*
Abbey Elizabeth Lunney*
Jordan Paige Lunney*
Kendall Katherine Lunney*
Bryce Maffet
Kendall Grace Maffet
Cara Cristina Maines*
William Christian Maines
Michelle Maresh
Lauren Keslye Marsh*
Lindsay Elyse Marsh*
Blake Masterson
Drew Masterson
Kendall Masterson
Will & Zach Maxwell*
May Marrinan McCabe
Sadie Caldwell McCabe
Ellen McCloskey*
Mary Evans McCloskey*
Ellie McCoin
Will McCoin
Andrew McCulloch
Katie McCulloch
Sean Michael McDonnell
Ryan Michael McDonnell
Molly Catherine McGreevy
Hayley Ray McNeill*
Sam Middlebrooks*
Madison Kate Miller
Jack Mitchell*
Barrett Mize*
Brindley Mize*
Caroline Montgomery
Katherine Montgomery
William Montgomery
Joe F. Moore, III*
Katherine Lauraleen Moore*
Edward Morris*
Henry Morris*
Jackson Morris*
Kendrick Morris*
Caroline Elizabeth Moseley
James Bruce "Jamie" Moseley IV
Sinclair Mott

Annie Murski*
Katie Murski*
The Nelson Family
Diana Nevins
Kelsey Nibert*
Kendall Nibert
Samantha Marie Nolen
Matthew Novelli
Nicholas Novelli
Carter Pace*
Matthew Evan Parra
Alexei Ashby Passmore
Caroline Paterson*
Lindsay Paterson
Harry Patterson
Sara Patterson
Avery Patton*
Barbara Sandy Patton
Logan Patton*
Paige Patton*
Mary Katharine Payne*
William Payne*
David Lawren Penberthy
Jackson Pittman
Allyson Poujol
Jaclyn Poujol*
Michael David Poujol
Rachael Poujol
Avery Claire Prasher
Morgan Prasher
Victoria Nicole Pride*
Claire Kemper Putnam
Connor Woods Quinn*
Graham Patrick Quinn*
Caroline Leigh Ramirez*
Caroline Reasoner*
Eloise Reasoner
Matthew Reasoner
Olivia Reasoner
William Reasoner
Harrison Reid
Max Reid
The Thomas F. Reilly Family
The Paul Reinhardt Family
Olympia Ridge*
Paloma Ridge-Rojas*
Campbell Knox Ross*
David Rowe*
William Rowe
Georgie Rose Rowntree*
Noah Rowntree*
Audrey Leigh Sarver*
Sarah Elizabeth Sarver*
John Christopher "Jake" Schick*
Ryan Michael Schick*
Blaise Schuenemann
Thomas Schuenemann
Melissa Schwartz
Caroline Searight
Meredith Searight
William Searight
Morgan & Cory Selzer*
Cade Shanks
Nicole Shanks
Olivia Shanks
Sara Beth Shelton
Shelby York Shelton
Paloma Quinones Sierra
Abby Simpson
Kendall Simpson
Ann Singleton
Drayton Edward Small*
Kelsey Herald Smith*
Kirby Laurel Smith*
Allison Smith*
Braden James Smith
Joshua Charles Smith
Ross Smith
Roy Smith
Sarah Smith
Shepherd Day Smith
Britt Jacob Sobiesk
Regan Gabrielle Sobiesk*
Lexie and Jeb Spalding
Julianne Elizabeth Staine*

Jake Steen*
Annie Stephens
Louise Stephens
Sam Stephens
Bethany Caroline Stevens*
Bradley Thomas Stevens*
Connor Crosswell Stone
Emily Clare Stone
Henry MacLean Stone
James Story
Katie Story*
Sarah Story
Elizabeth Strange
Mason Strange*
Clayton "Clay" Hicks Stratton
Hunter Ford Stratton
Ty Carter Stubbs*
Caroline Suffield
Elizabeth Suffield
Katherine E. Summerlin
Georgia Grey Svrcek
Harrison Grace Svrcek
The Szymanski Family
Caroline Talbert*
Emily Talbert
Courtney, Jim Bob & Katie Taylor
Jean M. Tenison
The Fay School First Graders
The Fay School Third Graders
Tullis Cullen Thomas, IV*
Melissa Marie Thurmond*
Ann Tidwell
Carlton Anne Putzka Touchy*
Henry A. Toy
Katheryn A. Toy
The Traband Family
Louis Tronzo
Megan Tronzo
Jared Williams Trozzo
Payne Phillips Trozzo
Kristen Unterbrink*
Elly Untermeyer*
Alison Claire Utz
Grace Bowen Valerius
Lillian Sheldon Valerius
Carter Vann*
Joanna Lee Vaseliades
Peter Vaseliades
Ben Vaughan
Henry Vaughan*
Pete Vaughan
Peter Drennan Wade
Marynell Therese Ward
Gracey Wallace
Nathaniel Wallace
William Wallace
Claire Watson
Connor Reid Watson
Gray Turner Watson
Amy Waughtal*
Connor Waughtal*
Walker Waughtal*
The Wiggins Family
Griffin Andres Wilkins
Georgia Clair Williams
Anna Woodruff
Rachel Woodruff
Asha Elizabeth Worsham
Jesse Lee Worsham
Kathryn Anne Worsham
Samuel Price Worsham
Holly Yeager
Melanie Kate Yeager
John Ytterberg*
Will Ytterberg*
The Christopher Zook Family
Meg Zschappel*
Sarah Zschappel*

(*) denotes also submitted a
"What Do Critters Dream?" form

"What Do Critters Dream?" Contributors

The Junior League of Houston, Inc., wishes to thank the hundreds of children who provided ideas and inspiration for *Sweet Dreams Douglas*. Your creativity made Douglas' dreams a unique adventure.

Christopher Abib
Daniel Able
Matthew Ainbinder
Becky Aksamit
Lizzy Aksamit
Brice Alford
Leyan Alotaibi
Christopher Amoruso
Ellye Anderson
Kaitlyn Meredith Anderson
Sean Andrews
Maria Arteaga-Sachnik
Anne Marie Atmar
Erin Atmar
Michael Atmar
Nathan J. Avery
Charles Paxton Bacarisse
Ellie Bailes
Emily A. Baker
Emily Anderson Baker
Keenan Barazi
Zaid Barazi
Bronwyn Allyn Barnwell
Alexandra Bates
Chrissy Behr
Arya Bekhradi
Peyton Belchic
David Bell
Hunter Bell
Margaret Bell
Katrina Benson
Katherine Anne Berman
Kelly Bernard
Bradley Berry
Kathleen Bertram
Kayla Biar
Lindsey Bienski
Tyler Bienski
Brent Bishop
Shawn Bishop
Jason Jeko Blades
Rose Bleakley
Farris Blount
Joshua Blount
Christina Bodin
Mabry Bolin
Zoe Bond
Barrett Bostick
Emily Ann Boswell
Kate Boswell
Virginia Boswell
Blair Bou-Chebl
Maddy Elizabeth Bowen
Bridgette Bowers
Chase Bowers
Caroline Braun
Hannah Braun
Lindsay Braun
John J. Brennan, IV
John Brewster
Jessica Briggs
Abigail Broussard
Elizabeth Broussard
Kevin Brueggeman
Elizabeth Buckley
Isabel Bujosa
Heather Patricia Bullock
Allison Burch
Katie Burdine

Brennan Burns
Colin Burns
Emma Grace Butler
William Shaw Butler
Makenzie Butos
Christopher Butryn
Laura Caroline Byrd
Andrew Cafcalas, Jr.
Laynie Cafcalas
Amy Elizabeth Callender
Andrew Dean Callender
Claire Campbell
Emma Katherine Carr
Cami Carrasco
Gregory James Carter, II
Laura Ashley Carter
Carroll Cartwright
Stewart Cartwright
James Case
Michael Letsos Case
William S. Case
Kevin Cassidy
Catherine Grace Catechis
Van Alan Cates, Jr.
Annie Cathriner
Virginia Cathriner
Alexander Chae
Amanda Chancellor
Kimberly Chancellor
Elysse Chappell-Dolby
Michaela Chappell-Dolby
Lainey Chenoweth
Maddie Chenoweth
Morgan Chenoweth
Tucker Chenoweth
Aubrey Cherry
Courtney Christian
Kathleen Maria Cisarik
Michael James Cisarik
Sally Kathryn Cisarik
Albert William Clay, IV
Catherine Grace Clay
Daniel Clay
Ryan James Cleary
Morgan Clinkscales
Barrett Cloud
Dennis Clutter
Becca Cohen
Billy Cohen
Hannah Cohen
Kimberly Cohen
Ford Collier
Jack Collier, Jr.
Will Collier
Carson Cone
Paige Connell
Sarah Claire Conner
Claire Cooper
Morgan Cooper
Jillian Cordova
Margot Cordova
Howard F. Cordray, III
Lauren Covey
Joe Cozby
Callie Ann Craddock
Caroline Craddock
Cody Alan Craddock
Jack Craddock
Catherine Elizabeth Craft
Logan Craft
Lauren Crow
Ryan Crow
Jack Culwell
Kristen Cummins
Connor Cunningham
Ryne Cunningham
Shannon Cunningham
Troup Cunningham
Ricky Davies
Madeleine Daly
Victoria Daly
Caroline Frances Davis
Kayla Elizabeth Davis
Arlin Ley Dawson

Mary Elizabeth Coghlan Dawson
Thomas Rapier Dawson
Hannah Dean
Alec DelSota
Caroline Dew
Carter DeWalch
Sarah DeWalch
Taylor DeWalch
Madelyn Esther DeYoung
Dania Diab
Elliot Diesel
Vince DiMichele
Connor Dixon
Kasey Dixon
Sam Dixon
Helen Darden Dodd
Lexi Drusch
Brooke Drew
Morgan Drew
Luke Duroc-Danner
Sydney Duire
Andrew Dun, Jr.
Henry Dun
Lindsay Dun
Hudson Duncan
Andrew Dunlap
Allison Dyer
Carolyn Dyer
Emma Dyer
Freeman Dyer
John Darden "J.D." Dyer
Jessica Easter
Joey Edwards
V. Grace Edwards
W. Porter Edwards
Harrison Eilers
James Elam
Michaela Grace Ellis
Nikki Ellis
Austin Epler
Katie Ewing
Daniel Farley
Sarah Farley
David Farrier
Elizabeth Farrier
Andrew Faulk
Randy Faulk
Kelsey French
Elizabeth Field
Robert Field
Max Christopher Finkelstein
Emily Fishman
Lauren Marie Fitzgerald
Lindsey Flesch
Anna Claire Flynn
Bernard Connor Flynn
Mary Ragan Foley
Haley Foster
Blake Fox
Cameron Fox
Joseph Francisco
Mabry Franklin
Derek Fry
Alexandra Gabitto
Sara Jane Gage
William Gage
Carly Gamson
John Ganucheau
Mary Clare Ganucheau
Mollie Gaylor
Jordy Geiler
Maggie Geiler
Elizabeth Gentry
Mia Gerachis
Max Gerson
Alexander Ghadially
Julian Ghadially
Gray Welch Gilbert
Jack Joseph Gilbert
Zoe Elizabeth Gillies

Reghan Gillman
Georgia Ginn
Margaret Ginn
Michael J. Glasser
Arman Gonzalez
Denton Graham
Lauren Graham
Turner Graham
Parker Grainger
James Hayden Grant
Sarah Nicole Grant
Harris Green
Drake Greenwood
Jimmy Greenwood
Lauren Greenwood
Courtney Greer
Griffith Greer
Tye Griffith
Lauren Renee Grimes
Nicolette Groen
Christina Gross
Samantha Grubb
Orry Gunay
Sebi Gutierrez
Mary Elizabeth Hale
Frances Carolyn Hamilton
Grace Elizabeth Hamilton
Henry Hamilton
Madeleine Janes Hamilton
Katherine Hampton
Claire Elizabeth Hamrick
James William Hamrick
Perla B. Haney-Jardine
Maggie Hansen
Adam Harmon
Daniel Harrison
Parker Harrison
Anna Grace Hawkins
John Heard
Moody Heard
Harland John Hebert
Quinn Joseph Hebert, Jr.
Hayden Held
Hayden Maria Henderson
Marshall Henry
Katherine Herbert
Hannah Herrold
Hunter Herzfield
Lauren Hewell
Clare Hewitt
Lauren Frances Heyne
James Hiester
Brittany Hildebrand
Sean Hildreth
Kacy Hill
Eric Hobby
Walker Hobby
Grace Hodo
Hannah Hodo
Bruce Hoefer
Grace Hoefer
Hayley Louise Hoefer
Karl Ernst Hoefer, Jr.
Margaux Hoefer
Rebecca Hoffman
Maghan Horne
Charlie Howell
Kendall Elisabeth Hudgens
Meredith Marie Hughes
James Hunsaker
Alden Hurst
John Ikenberry
Kathryn Ikenberry
Scott Jacobs
Noah Jamail
Megan Jamieson
Courtney Jenkins
Kyle Jenkins
Alexandra Jimenez
Carter Johnson

Julia Johnson
Sydney Johnson
Connor Jones
Craig Jones
Elise Jones
John Michael Jones
Jordan Jones
Kyle Judah
Mason Kallina
Grace Caroline Kaplow
Burdette Taylor Keeland
Bowden Kelly
Justin Kelly
Ford Kemp
Marten Kendrick
Andrew Kennedy
Katherine Kennedy
Madeleine Kennedy
Peter Kennedy
Alex Kerensky
Elizabeth Ann Kettler
Anna A. Khan
Sarah Khan
Thomas Wayne Kielman
Leslie Kimmons
Bryson King
Manda Kroll
Nicole Casey Krouse
Avery Kumpas
Michael Kumpas
Katherine Kuntz
Lyndsey Lafitte
Lindy Lamme
Maddox Lamme
Wil Langenstien
Elizabeth Larkin
Alexandra Leary
Perry Lee
Claire LeFevers
Caroline Leszinske
Charlotte Leszinske
Elizabeth Ann Liesse
Emma Lisanti
Sarah Livesay
Cameron Longer
Allie Lovell
Jacy K. Luedde
Addison Camille Lynch
Emily Marie Lynch
Holt Madden
Phillip Madden
Katherine Magliolo
Alex Mallard
Camilla Manca
Marcus Manca
Colette Mark
Cameron Alan Maresh
Lindsay Marsh
Emily Bolling Marsteller
Mary Alice Martin
Molly Martin
Russell Martin
Timmy Mashinski
Cody Mason
Wills Masterson
Meg Mathias
Tony Matta, III
Emily Taylor Matteson
Sara Blair Matthews
Ava McBath
Ryan McCleary
Madeline McDonald
Georgia Hargus McHenry
Matthew Strake McHenry
Robert Kingsley McHenry
Conor McKinney
Amanda Lee McLamb
Jack McNamara
Paige McNamara
Romy Megahed

Colin Mellinger
Adam Mendonca
Mark Walker Metyko
Mary Kathryn Metyko
Mathews Metyko
Maxwell Metyko
Emma Miertschin
Carolyn Taylor Miller
John Donelson Miller
Natalia Miller
S. Mitchell
John Montgomery
Elizabeth Katherine Moore
Angela Morisette
Jamie Moseley
Mackenzie Mott
Gabby Mueller
Grace Elizabeth Munford
Bill Munson
Trey Murphy
Matthew Alexander Murray
Jake Muth
Nicholas Spencer Myre
Mae Nasser
Hillary Neese
Jack Nelson
Abby Nevins
Blake Nevins
Darby Nevins
Wesley Notestine
Sarah Nyquist
Annie O'Boyle
Zachary Ogle
Meredith O'Neal
Jonathan Ong
Erinn Ormand
Kelsie Mika Osato
Gabrielle Otey
Katherine Padon
Connor Palmer
Anna Parkey
Will Parkey
Kate Patterson
Jack Pellegrin
Bennett Pepi
George Pepi
Lauren Perillo
Andrew Perry
Jay E. Peters
Mary Therese Pfeffer
Antoine Pierre Picou
Calvin Luke Picou, III
Lane Pleason
Andrew Porter
Hoyt Porter
Kayle Porter
Lundy Porter
Jackson Potter
Julia Potter
Madeleine Prator
Evelyn Pustka
Drew Putnam
Sam Putnam
Christian James Quinn
Colin Wilkinson Quinn
Meredith Meyer Rae
Marika Rafte
Madison Raley
Kara Ramer
Mallory Ramsey
Meredith Ramsey
Brandon Randall
Rachel Ransleben
Caroline Rao
Stephen Rao
Laura Rathmell
Christopher Rech
Megan Rech
Molly Anne Redepenning
Erica Ann Reed

Allison Rice
Annie Rice
Emily Rice
James Rice
Bennett Roach
Catherine Roach
Nicholas Robbins
Allie Robinson
Luke Robinson
Cali C. Roper
Caroline Ross
Cody Ross
Hayden Ross
Isabel Ross
Gianmarco Rossini
Ellie Rotan
Mac Rotan
Nina Rotan
Paul Rothenberg
Isabel Lee Ruch
Kelsey Russek
Reid Russek
Lacey Noelle Rybarczyk
Rylan Elizabeth Saleh
Tristan Randal Salinas
Aubrie M. Sanchez
Christine Sangalis
Austin Santhin
Dorothy Scarborough
Perry Schell
Thomas Daniel Schepmann
Abby Schroff
Scarborough Adelle Schlenker
Thomas Mabry Schlenker
Peter Schubert
Hilary Schuhmacher
Sarah Schuhmacher
Ashley Schwarz
Ava Manon Schweninger
Sam Seligmann
Harrison Seureau
Peter Seureau
Lovett Shaper
Nell Shaper
Ethan Shear
Patrick Sheehy
Cameron Marie Shepherd
John C. Shepherd, Jr.
Sarah Edwards Shepherd
Abbey Renee Shockley
Emmie Siegel
Samantha Siegler
Abigail Smith
Bennett Smith
Brenna Nicole Smith
Claire Smith
Julie Smith
Katherine Smith
Maddison Maree Smith
Nicholas Smith
Sassy Smith
Madeline Sneed
Adelaide Snell
Kyle Somers
Abby Spalding
Victoria Stanley
Susannah E. Starkey
Stacy Steinberger
Ann Katherine Stephens
Ellen Taylor Stephens
Kelli Stienke
Julia Ann Streller
Timmy Streller
Margaret Strode
Lexie Taggart
Michael Ian Davidson Taggart
Caroline Brooke Taylor
Catherine Paige Taylor
Taylor Wilby
Claire J. Thomas

Elaine Thomas
Elizabeth Thomas
Holly Thomas
Jasmine Thomas
Cyrus Thompson
Evie Thompson
Sara Thompson
Julianna Tidwell
Kendall Tillman
Vance Tillman
Candace Ting
Jessica Todd
Alex Tokoi
Matthew Tomberlin
Lexi Trauber
Alexis Christiana Trippon
Laura Turner
Philip Turpin
Ainsley Christine Vail
Alexandra Vaio
Brett Vaio
Kylie Valentine
Claire D. Valera
Cameron Van Cleave
Eric van Doesburg
Ashley Elizabeth Vaughan
Ashton Waddle
Kylie Wade
Georgia Wahl
Natalie Wahl
Henry T. Waite
Kirby Walker
Margaret Warmington
Meagan Walsh
Eric Franklin Wasserzug
Isabel Marie Wasserzug
Lyndsey Watson
Griffin Watt
Mitchell Webber
Julie Wegmann
Drew Weitzel
Erin Weitzel
Morgan Elizabeth Wenske
Elizabeth Carroll "Libby" Weyel
Foster Edward Weyel
Harrison Church Weyel
Taylor Weylandt
Thomas Whalen
Gregory Wiatrek
Katherine Wiatrek
Brooke Wiggins
James Wilby
Cordelia Claire Penn Wilcox
James Simpson Wilcox, IV
Mathilde Conway Farrell Wilcox
Warren Grant Wilder
Colin Williams
Marshall Wilson
Nicholas Harfield Wilson
Sean Ryan Wilson
Tara Wilson
Ashley Lynn Wood
Whitney Woodard
Ashley Woolie
Carson Yeager
Will Zaleski
Laura Zdunkewicz
Chrisoper Alan Zook, Jr.

Special Friends

The Junior League of Houston, Inc., wishes to thank the many friends, schools and businesses who, by their participation, have made this book possible. We are grateful for your enthusiasm, expertise, support, and generous donations.

Sarah Almy
Lower School Art Teacher,
River Oaks Baptist School

Jeanne Alsup
English Department Chair,
The Kinkaid School

Doug Bishop
Bishop & Heintz, P.C.

Melanie Blair's 2nd Grade Class
River Oaks Baptist School

Dana Brown's 1st Grade Class
The Kinkaid School

Caro Ann Germann
Lower School Librarian,
The Kinkaid School

Michelle Query Herrera
2001-2002 Cookbook Chairman

The 2001-2002 Cookbook Committee

Kathy Hobson, Librarian
Wilchester Elementary School

Marlene Isbell
The House at Pooh Corner

Jerry Jenkins
Jenkins Group, Inc.

Nancy Kelley
The House at Pooh Corner

Laurel's Catering, Inc.
Laurel Thompson

Aline Leporati Means

Gail Modrall
Librarian, Presbyterian School

Cecilia O'Connell's 3rd Grade Class
The Kinkaid School

Pesce
Johnny Carrabba and Family

Lauri Sack
Children's Chapters

Susan Mayfield Catering
Susan Mayfield

Helen Vietor
The House at Pooh Corner

Cindy Wilcoxon's 4th Grade Class
The Kinkaid School

Professional Credits

Concept, Design, and Art Direction
HILL Strategic Brand Solutions

Author/Illustrator
Regan Dunnick

Advisory Committee
Rick Barongi
Director
Houston Zoological Gardens

Sara Hickman
Singer/Songwriter

Tammie Kahn
Executive Director,
The Children's Museum of Houston

Bruce D. Perry, M.D., Ph.D.

Holly Shimizu
Executive Director,
United States Botanic Garden

Ron Stone
President, Stonefilms of Texas, Inc.

Chase Untermeyer
Texas State Board of Education, 1999-2003

The Junior League Of Houston, Inc. Presidents

2001-2002
Francel "Franny" Coleman Gray

2002-2003
Karen Koonce Ytterberg

Steering Committee

Chairman
Katherine "Kathy" Mitchell Abib

Publishing Director
Veronica "Roni" Obermayer Atnipp

Sustaining Advisor
Malinda Russek Crain

Assistant Chairman and Marketing Director
Julia Collier Humphreys

Concept/Design Coordinator
Tany Hopper James

Development Director
Trisha Anderson Mohle

Marketing Coordinator
Rebecca Penberthy Clark

Production Coordinator and
Pre-sales Coordinator
Amy Bredthauer Gissel

Sales Development Director
Jennifer Palmer Abney

Sales and Production Finance Manager
Teresa Lazzeri Maines

Special Events Coordinator
Courtnay Tartt Elias

Sustainer Committee

Nancy O'Connor Abendshein
Nancy Sellingsloh Bertin
Susan Heyn Billipp
Boone Boies Bullington
Catherine Choate Christopherson
Terry Hastings Dean
Anne Pearce French
Stephanie Goldfield
Gail Braden Goodwin
Beverle Gardner Grieco
Carolyn Burton Hamilton
Carol Jones Hoppe
Clare Wiggins Jackson
Josie Shanks Jones
Susan Ray Mayfield
Jacqueline "Jackie" Gilbert McCauley
Cara Okoren Moczulski
Julie Stone Payne
Anne Elizabeth Wise Pullen
Laura Griffin Schuhmacher